Wake Up, Little One!

For my cousin Helen, with love
~ C F

To my niece, Ella Victoria Wernert
~ T M

Originally titled *One Magical Day*

ISBN-13: 978-0-545-04191-1
ISBN-10: 0-545-04191-0

12 11 10 9 8 7 6 5 4 3 2   8 9 10 11 12/0
Printed in the U.S.A.   40

First Scholastic printing, October 2007

Wake Up, Little One!

Originally titled
One Magical Day

Claire Freedman   Tina Macnaughton

SCHOLASTIC INC.
New York Toronto London Auckland Sydney
Mexico City New Delhi Hong Kong Buenos Aires

Night shadows fade
to a pale, golden dawn.
It's a magical day –
wake up, Little Fawn!

Mother Duck wakens
her brood with a kiss.
This beautiful morning
is too good to miss!

Up in the poppy field
frisky lambs play,
Skipping with joy
on this new summer's day.

Small piglets scamper
and skip in the sun;
Rolling in mud
is such squelchy fun!

Warm breezes drift
down the flower-filled lanes,
Where fluffy-tailed puppies
run 'round, playing games.

Into the stable
the warm sunlight streams,
Bathing the foal
with its soft, golden beams.

Sun-drowsy kittens
pad home to their mother.
Washed one by one,
they curl up with each other.

Happy and free,
the wild swallow weaves,
Then swoops to her nest,
built high in the eaves.

Little calves rest
in the shade of the trees,
Where butterflies dance
on the fresh, gentle breeze.

Donkey nods off
in the last patch of sun.
Softly the light fades;
the day's almost done.

Blinking in wonder,
two shy fox cubs peep,
As deep in the meadow,
the long shadows creep.

Stars shine like diamonds,
the full moon gleams bright,
Gently Owl hoots –
it's a magical night!